A Midsummer Night's Dream

Written by John Dougherty

Illustrated by Manuel Sumberac

Collins

Characters, in order of appearance:

Theseus, Duke of Athens: ruler of the city.

Hippolyta, Queen of the Amazons: engaged to be married to Theseus.

Demetrius: a young nobleman. Was engaged to Helena. Now wants to marry Hermia instead.

Helena: a friend of Hermia. In love with Demetrius.

Egeus: an Athenian lord.

Hermia: daughter of Egeus. In love with Lysander.

Lysander: another young nobleman. In love with Hermia.

Moth: a fairy. Servant to Queen Titania.

Puck: another fairy. Servant to King Oberon.

Titania: the fairy queen.

Quince: Bottom's friend and director of the play.

Oberon: the fairy king.

Nick Bottom: a terrible amateur actor. Wants to perform a play for Theseus's royal wedding.

Flute and Snug: Bottom's friends and fellow actors.

3

Chapter 1

Theseus, duke of the city of Athens, was in a good mood. In four days, he was going to marry the brave and beautiful Queen Hippolyta. He'd just given the order for all of Athens to take the week off and start celebrating. And now he was taking his bride-to-be out into the city, to spend the morning showing off about how much his people loved him.

His good mood didn't, however, last for long. Scarcely had he and Hippolyta stepped out of his palace when ...

"Duke Theseus! Your Grace!"

Theseus turned to see who'd spoken, and sighed quietly. It was Egeus, one of the noble lords of the city, and he didn't look happy. With him was a young woman, who appeared to be equally lacking in the happiness department, and two young men. One of the young men was clearly just as unhappy as everyone else, and the other looked – well, a bit smug, really.

Theseus sighed again. It looked as if he was going to have to spend the morning listening to people's problems. Honestly, sometimes he felt less like a duke and more like everybody's best friend – although, unlike ordinary best friends, he did at least have the power to have people put to death if they got really irritating.

"What's the problem, Egeus?" Theseus asked. He wasn't really looking forward to the answer, but at least, he thought, with a smile at Hippolyta, it might give him the chance to show her how good he was at being wise.

Egeus needed no more encouragement than that. "Your Grace, I'm extremely cross with my daughter Hermia!" He indicated the young woman, who folded her arms stroppily and glared at her father. "I've gone to a great deal of trouble to arrange a marriage for her," Egeus continued, "and I've chosen young Demetrius."

At this, the smug young man looked even more smug, and bowed to the duke.

"I think he'll make an excellent husband for my daughter, I really do. But Lysander here ..." At this point, he glanced coldly at the other young man, who avoided his gaze and looked unhappily at the pavement.

"Lysander has tricked my daughter into falling in love with him! It's outrageous! He's craftily written poems for her, and sneakily given presents to her and cunningly sat outside her window singing soppy songs to her, and deviously fooled her into loving him, and now she won't marry Demetrius when I say she has to!"

Egeus paused for breath, but not quite for long enough to give anyone else a chance to interrupt.

"So, your Grace," he went on, "I've brought Hermia to you in order to give her one last chance. I'd like her to tell you that she's very sorry she's been naughty, and that she's going to do as Daddy says and marry Demetrius. If she won't, then I'd like you to please let me kill her."

For a moment, Theseus wasn't sure what to say. On the one hand, Egeus did have a point. According to Athenian custom, a daughter was her father's property, and he was allowed to tell her who to marry; if she refused then, technically, yes, he was allowed to have her killed. But on the other hand, Theseus didn't really think fathers *should* go around killing their daughters. It wasn't a nice way to behave. He stole another glance at Hippolyta and decided he was going to have to be very wise indeed.

"What do you say, Hermia?" he asked. "You really should obey your father, you know. Demetrius is a good choice."

Hermia looked him in the eye. "So is Lysander," she replied.

Theseus decided that he rather liked Hermia. He approved of the confident yet respectful way she spoke to him. If it were up to him, he'd tell her to ignore her whiny father and marry whoever she liked.

But even a duke couldn't ignore the law. Otherwise his people might start ignoring it too, and go around saying naughty words and murdering each other. He had to come up with a clever plan.

9

Then it came to him. He drew himself up to his full height, put on his wisest and most dukely expression, and in his dukeliest voice said, "You have a choice, Hermia. You can do what your father says and marry Demetrius."

At this, Demetrius looked horribly pleased with himself.

"Or," Theseus went on, rather wishing he was talking to Demetrius and not Hermia, "you can die."

Hermia looked at him bravely. Clearing his throat, he continued. "Or," he said, "you can become a nun." He paused, enjoying everyone's puzzled expressions. "Of course," he added, "if you take the nun option, that means you can't ever get married. To anyone. So you probably won't like it. But I expect it's better than being dead."

"Your Grace," Hermia began, "in that case, I must choose ..."

Theseus held up his hand for silence. This was the clever bit; the bit he was really proud of. "Don't tell me now. Have a think about it. Come back in ... let's say, four days. That's my wedding day, as you know. If you decide to marry Demetrius, we can have a double wedding. But if you decide to die or become a nun, well, we can have someone make the arrangements. OK?"

And that might have been the end of it, if Demetrius hadn't decided to start an argument.

"Be sensible, Hermia," he said. "Marry me. It's better than being dead or becoming a nun. And Lysander, give up, why don't you? I'm her dad's favourite."

"If Hermia's dad loves you so much, Demetrius," Lysander replied coolly, "why don't you marry him, and let me marry Hermia?"

Now, that was funny, Theseus thought, just managing to turn his snigger into a cough.

Egeus wasn't amused. "Yes," he said, "I *do* like Demetrius more!"

More fool you, thought Theseus.

"Your Grace," Lysander said, turning to the duke, "I'm as good a man as Demetrius is. If money's what Egeus is worried about, my family's at least as well-off as his. And I love Hermia more than Demetrius does, and more importantly, she loves me! Besides," he added with a scowl, "I'm more loyal than him. Not so long ago, he went around telling Helena – Hermia's friend – that he loved her, until she fell in love with him. Then he dropped her and went chasing after Hermia, leaving poor Helena heartbroken!"

"Yes," said Theseus thoughtfully, wondering how he could bring this conversation to a close, "I'd heard about that. Tell you what – Egeus and Demetrius, come and walk with Hippolyta and me for a few minutes. Let's see if I can come up with some wise advice for you."

He took Hippolyta's hand and strolled off into the city, with Egeus and Demetrius following.

And if Hermia and Lysander have any sense, he thought, *as soon as they're alone, they'll decide to run away together.*

Chapter 2

"I know!" said Lysander, as soon as they were alone. "Let's run away together! I've got an aunt who lives about 20 miles away from Athens. The laws are different there, and they're not quite so keen on forcing people into marriages and killing daughters." As Hermia's eyes lit up with sudden hope, he continued, "You know that place in the woods where we went for a picnic with Helena? Let's meet there tomorrow night, go straight to my aunt's house and get married!"

"Brilliant!" Hermia agreed. "Let's do it. I'll meet you there tomorrow night – I promise."

They smiled at each other, and then they started doing all that soppy stuff that people do when they're in love, like calling each other "sweetie-pie" and "dumpling" and "fluffy pumpkin".

They were still doing this when Helena rounded the corner
and bumped into them.

"Oh!" said Hermia, startled. "Helena! I'm so glad to see you!"
She stepped forward to give her friend a hug.

Helena stepped back and folded her arms angrily. "Don't you touch me,
you ... you ... you *heart-stealer*!"

Hermia's face fell. "Helena, that's so unfair!" she protested.
"I didn't steal anybody's heart!"

"Oh, really?" Helena snapped. "Then how come Demetrius dropped me and went chasing after you? You must've done *something* to make him pay attention to you!"

"I didn't do anything!" Hermia insisted. "It's Lysander I love! I don't even *like* Demetrius! I keep telling him that, and ignoring him and glaring at him, but he just keeps following me around!"

Tears welled in Helena's eyes. "And I keep telling Demetrius I love him, and saying nice things to him and smiling at him, but he just keeps running away from me!"

Hermia's heart almost broke at her friend's sorrow. She glanced at Lysander; he nodded agreement.

"Helena," she said, "don't be sad. Lysander and I are going to run away."

"Yes," Lysander said, "tomorrow night."

Helena looked suspiciously from one to the other, as if afraid some cruel joke was being played upon her.

"It's true!" Hermia insisted. "We're going to meet in the woods after dark. We're going to leave Athens and run away to get married. Maybe when I'm gone, Demetrius will fall in love with you again, Helena. I hope so. Wish us luck!"

She turned to Lysander and grinned at him. "See you tomorrow!" she whispered, before running lightly for home.

Lysander smiled at Helena. "Good luck, Helena," he said, "With Hermia and me gone from Athens, I hope Demetrius will love you again."
Then he, too, was gone.

Helena watched them go, and her heart was gripped by bitterness. *Even if Demetrius does marry me now,* she thought, *I'll always know I was second best. It's not fair. Why should Hermia get to live happily ever after, if I don't?*

And since jealousy can make us foolish, perhaps it's not surprising that her next thought was: *But if I tell Demetrius that Hermia's going to run away, perhaps at last he'll see that she doesn't deserve him – and I do!*

Chapter 3

The ghostly moon rose high and full over the Athenian wood. Its eerie brightness cast strange shadows in the clearings and among the trees.

If Hermia and Lysander hadn't been so desperate, perhaps they wouldn't have chosen tonight to make their escape. For this was Midsummer Night, one of the most magical nights of the year, and they were not alone in the woods. As they ran together through a moonlit glade, someone was watching them. Her name was Moth.

She was a fairy; a creature of magic and enchantment.

Like all of her kind, she was invisible to

human eyes.

As Hermia and Lysander disappeared into the shadows of the wood, Moth saw another fairy step out from between the trees. He was a merry little fellow with a mischievous face, and clothed all in green and red.

"Hello, fairy!" he said cheerily. "How's it going?"

Moth smiled. "It's busy!" she said. "I'm just getting this clearing ready for the fairy queen. She'll be here soon."

The little fellow's cheeky smile slipped a little. "Ah," he said. "We might have a problem there. *I've* been sent to get this particular glade ready for the fairy *king*. And I don't know if you've heard, but King Oberon isn't very happy with Queen Titania just at the moment. They've had a huge row, and the king is furious. If I were you, I'd make sure the queen stays away."

"I thought I recognised you!" Moth said. "You're Puck, aren't you?
The king's mischief-maker?"

Puck grinned. "That's me," he said. "The best trickster there is.
I even make King Oberon smile sometimes, and that's not easy,
I can tell you. I'm a master of disguise, too, and ... Oh, look out;
here's the king!"

"Ah," said Moth, dismayed. "And here's
the queen, too. That's bad timing."

The temperature in the glade seemed to drop by several degrees as King Oberon and Queen Titania glared at each other.

"What are you doing here?" Oberon asked coldly.

"I might ask the same of you," Titania retorted. "After all, I was here first."

"I think you'll find that I was here first, actually."

They glared at each other some more, while their servants fidgeted uncomfortably.

"Well," said Titania eventually, "if you're staying here, I'm leaving. It's a big wood, and I'm sure we can find somewhere well away from you to enjoy ourselves. Come on, Moth."

She turned and swept majestically from the clearing, giving Oberon one last frosty stare as she left.

"Oh, that woman," Oberon growled.

"She makes me so cross!" He paused,
a cunning smile creeping on to his face.

"What she needs, Puck, is one of your tricks!"

Puck grinned, and bowed before his king.

"Just tell me what to do, boss."

Oberon smiled, stroking his beard thoughtfully.

"Do you remember where we were sitting the other
month when we saw that mermaid?" Puck nodded.

"Did you notice some little purple flowers growing nearby?"

"I did," Puck answered.

"Well," the king told him, "I want you to fetch me a couple,
and be quick about it. I know it's a long way, but ..."

"For you, boss," Puck said, "I'll go right round the world in
40 minutes!"

And then he wasn't there anymore.

Oberon smiled to himself. Then a noise nearby made him turn his head. A young man and a young woman had stepped into the clearing.

They didn't see Oberon. It's part of the magic of the fairy folk that no human can see or hear a fairy, unless that fairy chooses to be seen or heard. Oberon, however, could see and hear them and, curious, he watched and listened.

"Stop following me, Helena!" the young man said, with a sneer that looked both angry and ... well, a bit smug, really.

"Why are you so mean, Demetrius?" whined the young woman. "If I hadn't told you about their plan, you wouldn't even know Hermia and Lysander were running away!"

"Yeah? Well, where are they, then?" Demetrius snapped. "I can't see them, can you? You're useless, you are. Just clear off! I don't need you following me about!"

"You said you loved me!" protested Helena.

"And now I've changed my mind!" Demetrius said. "Just get lost. If you don't stop following me, I'm going to run off into the woods and hide, and then you'll get eaten by wild animals, and I won't care!"

And with that, Demetrius ran off into the woods, with Helena following at his heels.

As Oberon watched them go, Puck returned to the clearing.

"Here you are, boss," he said, holding up the purple flowers. "Do you mind if I ask what you want them for?"

Oberon took the flowers, and held them up in the moonlight. "These flowers, Puck," he said, "are very rare, and very special. If you squeeze one, and drop its juice in someone's eyes, they'll fall in love with the next creature they see."

Puck's eyes widened with delight. "You could have fun with that!"

"Precisely," Oberon said. "Now, later tonight my queen will want to sleep. When she does, I'll find her and drop some of this magical flower juice on her eyes. And when she wakes up, she'll fall in love with whatever she sees first – whether it's a lion, or a bear, or a wolf, or even a monkey!"

Puck threw his head back and laughed. "Oh, that's funny! I can't wait to see what happens!" Then his forehead wrinkled. "Wait a minute, boss. Don't you think, maybe, after a few years, you might get a little tired of your wife being in love with a monkey?"

"Fear not, Puck," Oberon said. "I know a magical song that will undo the effects of this potion. I'll use this charm when I decide the queen has learnt her lesson."

Puck chuckled mischievously. "Good one, boss! Hey – can I play a trick on someone with the magic flower, too?"

"Funny you should say that," Oberon replied. "There's a young man in this wood – Demetrius by name – who needs to be taught a lesson. You'll recognise him by his clothing – he's dressed in the latest Athenian fashions. With him is a young woman called Helena, who seems very sweet, if a bit whiny. It seems that he told her he loved her, and then changed his mind."

Puck shrugged. "These things happen, boss," he said.

"True," Oberon agreed. "But he doesn't need to be so cruel about it. So," he continued, handing one of the purple flowers back to Puck, "I'd like you to find him, preferably when he's asleep, and squeeze some of the juice on to his eyes. Make sure Helena is nearby, so that he sees her as soon as he wakes. That way, Demetrius will be even more in love with Helena than she is with him."

Puck grinned a mischievous grin. "My pleasure, boss," he said. And in an instant, he was gone.

Oberon smiled to himself, and looked once more at the magical flower. *And now*, he thought, *to play a little trick on that stubborn wife of mine!*

Chapter 4

There was a place in the Athenian wood where the wild flowers grew tall.
Their perfume sweetened the air and their pretty heads nodded gently in
the breeze. This was where King Oberon found his wife. Her fairy servants
had sung her to sleep, and then tiptoed away to play in the woods.
Titania was quite alone, and there was no need to watch over her.
No human could see her unless she chose to be seen, and no animal
would dare to harm her.

The servants hadn't considered, however, that they should be
on guard against the queen's own husband.

Moving as silently as only a fairy can, Oberon crept to where Titania lay. He squeezed some magical juice from the flower on to first one eyelid, and then the other. Then, satisfied, he moved quietly away.

I'll find Puck, he thought, and tell him to come and keep watch. He can tell me when Titania wakes. When she falls in love with some wild animal with no manners, no dress sense, and no ability to write love poetry, that'll teach her to argue with her husband!

The wild woods have a magic of their own that often leads travellers astray. Perhaps that is why, elsewhere in the wood, Hermia and Lysander weren't finding things easy.

"I was sure my aunt's house was this way," Lysander said, scratching his head. "But this path doesn't seem right."

"I think we might have been this way already," said Hermia. "This clearing looks awfully familiar."

"Really?" Lysander looked around, puzzled. "I'm sorry, my love. I've been to my aunt's house dozens of times before – I don't know why it's so difficult tonight."

The trees rustled their leaves. It sounded oddly like quiet laughter.

"Don't apologise, Lysander," Hermia said. "I'd rather be lost in the woods with you than with anyone else."

Lysander smiled soppily. "Me, too," he replied; then they started into all the "sweetiekins" and "dumpling" and "fluffy pumpkin" stuff again. It went on for quite some time. Eventually, Hermia gave a little yawn.

"Oh, I'm sorry, my little snuggle-bucket," Lysander said. "You must be exhausted. Shall we have a short nap here?" He sat down on the floor. "It's comfier than you'd think."

Hermia sat down beside him. "Oh, yes – the moss is all sort of soft and spongy." She lay down, curling herself up. "Yes, I think I might be able to ... um ... nyuh ... er ..." And then she was asleep.

Lysander lay down next to her, and wriggled uncomfortably. A tree root was digging into his back. With a weary groan, he crawled away, finding a more comfortable space not far from Hermia, and within seconds he, too, was asleep.

They were still fast asleep when a small figure dressed in green and red stepped into the clearing and stumbled upon the sleeping Lysander.

"Ah-hah!" Puck chuckled to himself. "What's this? A young man, wearing the latest Athenian fashions! You'll be Demetrius, then. I've been looking for you." He gazed around the clearing and caught sight of Hermia. "And you must be young Helena! Going by what the king said, my dear, you deserve better than this rat bag. Still, if you want him – you can have him!"

With a mischievous laugh, Puck squeezed several drops of the magical flower juice into Lysander's eyes. "Demetrius, mate," he whispered, bending so low that his nose almost touched the young man's, "when you wake up, you're going to be so in love!"

With a merry skip, he disappeared into the trees.

Moments later, Helena ran into the clearing. "Demetrius!" she was calling. "*Demetrius!* Come back!"

In her distress, she wasn't really looking where she was going, which is probably why she tripped over Lysander.

"Eeeeeeeeeeeeee!" Helena shrieked and then, recognising him in the moonlight, she squealed, "*Lysander!*"

"Uh?" Lysander answered sleepily, and woke up.

He could not have known it, of course, but this was a very bad idea. The juice of the magical flower was still fresh upon his eyes, and when he opened them the first thing he saw was ... Helena. Instantly, he fell deeply, and quite ridiculously, in love.

Helena quickly got to her feet. "Sorry!" she said. "Are you OK?"

"OK?" Lysander answered in a tone of wonder. "I'm *so* much better than OK, my little fluffy pumpkin!"

"Er ..." Helena began, puzzled, "I think Hermia's your little fluffy pumpkin, actually ..."

"Hermia?" Lysander almost spat the word. "Pah! Hermia's *boring*! I don't know what I ever saw in her! She's nothing compared to you, my Helena, my lovey-dovey sugar pie, my gorgeous treacle pudding, my great big fluffy bunny-wunny!"

Helena's eyes narrowed suspiciously. "Is this some kind of joke? Oh, I get it! You think it's funny that Demetrius doesn't want to marry me! You don't think *anyone* would want to marry me, and you're making fun of me!"

Lysander stepped towards her. "I'm not, Helena!" he said. "I don't know what I was ever thinking of, running away with Hermia when all along, there you were – more lovely than ... than ... than swirly caramel ice-cream topped with marshmallows and chocolate sauce and everything! Oh, run away with me! Marry me!"

"Ewwww," Helena said. "No thanks. In fact ... I think you're horrid. How dare you pretend to love me when you're going to marry Hermia! You're worse than Demetrius!"

And with that, she turned and fled.

"Helena! My true love!" Lysander cried, and – with no thought for Hermia, his *real* true love – chased after her.

Perhaps it was the magic of the wild woods that had made Hermia's sleep so deep that none of this woke her. And perhaps it was that same magic that woke her now, just as the sound of Lysander's running footsteps faded away. She yawned; stretched; looked around ...

... and realised she was alone.

"Lysander?" she called, worriedly. "Lysander?"

There was no answer.

Lysander would never have left me alone in these dark woods, she thought. *Perhaps something bad has happened to him! I must find him!*

Then another thought struck her. *And if Demetrius has anything to do with this, I'll make him wish he'd never been born!*

Chapter 5

Puck, meanwhile, had come upon the flowery glade where Queen Titania lay sleeping.

Best be quiet, he thought, creeping away. *It'd never do to wake her up and have her fall in love with me! That'd be a bit awkward!*

A noise made him pause. *Now, what's that? Sounds like more humans to me.*

As Puck stepped lightly through the trees, the voices grew louder. Before long, he'd entered another clearing in the woods, where four men stood talking.

"This is going to be the best play in all of Athens,
or my name's not Nick Bottom!" one of them – a large,
round-bellied man with a red nose – was saying.
"Every night from now until the duke's
wedding day, we're going to practise it in
secret, out here in the woods. That way
nobody can steal our ideas. Now, Quince –
tell us who's playing each part."

Quince stood, and took out
a sheaf of paper.
"Right," he said.
"Bottom, you're
playing Pyramus."

"Lovely," said Bottom.
"I'll be a really good Pyramus.
I'll be the best Pyramus ever.
I'll be absolutely fantastic
at being Pyramus.
Who *is* Pyramus?"

"Pyramus," said Quince,
"is a man."

"Great," said Bottom.
"I'm really good at being a man.
What about the others?"

"Let me see," said Quince, turning back to the front page. "Flute's going to be Thisbe. She's a lady."

"I can't be a lady!" Flute protested. "I've got a beard!"

"I could be the lady, too," Bottom offered. "I could stand on one side of the stage and be Pyramus, and then I could run over to the other side and be the lady. I could speak in a squeaky voice and everything."

"You can't be the lady," Quince said. "You're being Pyramus. Flute's being Thisbe. And Snug's being a lion."

"I could be the lion as well," Bottom suggested. "I'm great at roaring. I could roar really quietly so I don't scare the audience."

"You can't be the lion," Quince said wearily. "You're being Pyramus. Now, let's get on with it. Go and stand outside the clearing, and I'll tell you when to come on."

Puck, hidden from human eyes and ears, chuckled. "What a bunch of fools!" he said to himself. "Especially the red-nosed guy. He's got no more sense than a donkey." His face split into a huge and playful grin. "Now there's an idea! Time for some of my special magic!" He slipped off into the darkness after Bottom.

"Right," said Quince. "Flute, you come on, and say, 'Pyramus! O Pyramus!'"

Flute shuffled awkwardly on to the stage. "Pyramus. O Pyramus," he muttered.

"HERE I AM, MY LOVE!!!" Bottom roared, striding out from between the trees. His friends froze in horror. They recognised his voice. They recognised his clothing. They recognised the way his belly hung over his belt. But they didn't recognise Bottom's face – because his face was gone. In fact, his whole head was gone. In its place, sitting on Bottom's neck as though it had always been there, and speaking with Bottom's voice, was the head of a donkey.

There was silence. Quince, Flute and Snug stared. They stared some more. They kept staring, their mouths open in shock and disbelief. And then they found their voices.

"*AAAAAAAAAAAAAAAAAAAUGHHHHHHH!*" they yelled, and as they yelled, they ran. They ran faster than any of them had ever run, bumping into each other and into the trees in their haste to escape. Within seconds, their screams had faded away, and to Bottom's donkey-ears, there was no sound in the clearing at all.

The ears of a fairy, however, would have clearly heard from the darkness between the trees the sound of uncontrollable laughter. For Puck, overjoyed at the success of his joke, was lying in the shadows, clutching his sides as he howled with merriment.

As a confused Bottom stood in the clearing, another sound reached Puck's ears, and his eyes widened with delight. It was a voice he knew well, even if it was a little fuddled with sleep. It was saying: "What, may I ask, is the cause of all this noise?"

And as Puck watched gleefully, Queen Titania stepped into the clearing, took one look at the donkey-headed Bottom, and fell deeply, and quite ridiculously, in love.

This trickery, thought Puck, *is working out even better than I'd hoped for!*

Chapter 6

Queen Titania couldn't believe her eyes. Never had she seen such an enchanting creature. "Are you of fairy, or of human kind?" she asked.

The creature made no reply, but carried on staring bemusedly into the woods.

Human, then, since it can't see me, she thought, gazing upon it with wonder and admiration. She circled it, admiring the roundness of its belly; the long curve of its nose; the hairiness of its ears. Once she was behind it, she made herself visible to human eyes.

"Hello," she said softly.

Bottom turned, and jumped with surprise. Before him stood a beautiful lady, dressed in a gown of rich and shining silk. On her head sat a small crown which seemed to have been made out of silver flowers. She was clearly a noble lady, and she was smiling at him in a way that no other noble lady had ever smiled at him before.

"What's your name?" she asked.

"Er ... Bottom," said Bottom.

Queen Titania gasped. It seemed to her that she'd never heard such a beautiful name. "Bottom!" she said. "Never have I seen such a lovely Bottom. You must be the handsomest Bottom in the world. And from now on, you will be *my* Bottom!"

"Er ... right," said Bottom, wondering what was going on.

Titania stepped forward and stroked Bottom's nose. It felt a bit tickly, in a nice sort of way. "I'll order my servants to obey you!" she said. "And they'll bring you anything you ask for!"

Bottom still didn't quite understand what was going on, but the idea of being brought anything he asked for was very appealing. "Um ... Got any pancakes?" he said.

Puck had seen enough. He slipped away to find Oberon.

The king wasn't far off. "Well, Puck?" he said, as his servant appeared. "What news do you have for me?"

"You should've been there, boss! The queen's in love with a monster!" As Oberon's brow wrinkled in amused puzzlement, Puck explained: "I found a crew of daft Athenians practising a play in the woods, and the daftest one of all – well, I couldn't resist it. When he stepped out of sight of the others, I gave him ..."

Almost overwhelmed by a fit of the giggles, Puck took a deep breath, and tried again: "I gave him a donkey's head! And ... then the queen woke up and ... and ... *and fell in love with him!*"

Overcome by laughter, Puck collapsed in a heap, shaking and chortling
and beating the ground. Oberon couldn't help smiling.

"Well done, my Puck," he said. "I couldn't have planned it better!
And have you dealt with Demetrius, too?"

Recovering himself, Puck stood up, wiping his eyes. "Yes, boss,"
he said. "All sorted. I found him and Helena fast asleep, and dripped
a good dose of flower juice in his eyes. He should be completely in love
with her by now."

Just then, came the sound of approaching feet. "Look!" said Oberon. "Here comes Demetrius now!"

"Er ... no, boss," Puck said uncertainly, as Demetrius appeared, running through the trees. "That's not Demetrius. But that's Helena," he added, as Hermia, coming from another direction, caught sight of Demetrius and, yelling his name, ran for him.

"Demetrius!" she cried again, her voice furious. "Just as I thought! I *knew* I'd find you sneaking about these woods, up to no good! Where's Lysander? What have you done with him?"

Demetrius turned, surprised, just as Hermia, arms outstretched, pushed him over. He sprawled, surprised, against a tree. "What did you do that for?" he complained.

"What have you done with Lysander?" Hermia repeated. "He'd never have left me alone and asleep in the woods! What did you do to him? Have you kidnapped him?"

Demetrius stared up at her. "I don't know what you're talking about, Hermia," he said. "I don't know where Lysander is, and I don't care. Maybe he's run off with Helena. That'd suit me."

Hermia glared at him. "If I find you're lying ..." she said threateningly. "Oh – and don't even think about following me." With that, she turned and was gone.

Demetrius watched her go. "Yeah ... well ..." he muttered. "I won't follow you, then. But not because *you* said so. Just because I'm so tired. I've been wandering round in these woods for hours. I could do with a rest. Just for a couple of minutes ..."

His voice trailed away as he closed his eyes and instantly fell asleep.

Oberon gave Puck a sarcastic look. "You seem to have messed that up quite spectacularly," he said. "It looks as if you've dripped the magic flower juice into the wrong person's eyes."

Puck shrugged. "You said:
'A young man dressed in the latest
Athenian fashions.' How was I
to know there'd be two of them
running around the woods?"

"Well," said Oberon, "clearly,
there are. And my guess is, you've
made young Hermia's true
love – this Lysander – fall in love
with someone else. Which was
not the idea."

Puck shrugged again.
"Guess not." He grinned.
"Funny, though, isn't it?"

"Not really," said Oberon.

"Oh," said Puck. "Well, you're
the boss. What do you want me
to do about it?"

Oberon stroked his beard.
"Go and look for the real Helena,
and lead her here. I'll drip some
flower juice into Demetrius's eyes
before she gets here."

Puck grinned. "I'm on my way!"

He was back, minutes later. "Here she comes, boss!" he said. "I made myself look like Hermia, and let Helena see me running through the woods ahead of her. She followed me, all right. Only ..." He cleared his throat. "Only that other young man's running after *her*, begging her to marry him. So when Demetrius here wakes up, there'll be two of them both wanting to be her husband. That'll be funny, won't it?"

He glanced hopefully at Oberon. Oberon didn't look as though he thought it'd be funny at all.

"*Please*," panted Helena, staggering through the trees to where, unseen by her, the two fairy men stood. "Stop following me!"

"But I *love* you!" insisted Lysander.

"No you *don't*!" Helena said tearfully. "You love Hermia! Demetrius loves Hermia! *Everybody* loves Hermia, and nobody loves me. Can't you see how cruel you're being? It's horrible, pretending to be in love with me when you're not! Stop making fun of me!"

"I'm *not*!" insisted Lysander. "Oof!" he added, as he tripped over Demetrius, who was still fast asleep, and fell on him.

"Uh?" said Demetrius, waking. He looked up, saw Helena, and fell deeply, and quite ridiculously, in love. "Helena!" he said, pushing Lysander off him and getting to his feet. "My beloved!"

Helena stared at him in disbelief. "You awful, awful men!" she spluttered. "You're *both* making fun of me!"

Lysander furiously got to his feet and glared at Demetrius. "Are you making fun of my beloved?" he demanded.

"I'm not your beloved!" Helena snapped.

"See!" snarled Demetrius. "She's *not* your beloved! She's *my* beloved!"

"I'm not *your* beloved either, as well you know!" Helena shouted tearfully. "I wanted to be, but you went off after Hermia!"

"Hermia?" scoffed Demetrius. "Ha! Hermia means nothing to me!"

"Yeah?" said Lysander. "Well, Hermia means even less to me!"

"*What?*" said Hermia, in dismay. She'd heard the shouting and followed the noise; none of the others had seen her arrive. "How can you say that, Lysander? You love me!"

"Love *you?*" said Lysander scornfully. "That's rubbish! I love Helena!"

"But ..." gasped Hermia. "But ... you said I was your fluffy pumpkin!"

"*You're* not my fluffy pumpkin! *Helena's* my fluffy pumpkin!"

"I'm *not* your fluffy pumpkin!" Helena yelled, blushing.

"Yeah, Lysander!" Demetrius shouted. "Helena's not your fluffy pumpkin! She's *my* fluffy pumpkin!"

"Wait a minute!" Hermia said, thoroughly confused. "I thought you wanted *me* to be your fluffy pumpkin!"

"Nobody," yelled Lysander, "is *anybody's* fluffy pumpkin except Helena, who is *my* fluffy pumpkin!"

"But, Lysander," Hermia said, near to tears, "you'll always be *my* fluffy pumpkin!"

Oberon looked at Puck. "I'm getting a headache," he said.

"I," Lysander said to Hermia, "will never be anyone's fluffy pumpkin but Helena's."

Hermia stood for a moment, as if stunned. Then she turned to Helena. "You've ruined my life!" she shouted, and ran off into the darkness of the woods.

"Hermia!" Helena shouted, chasing after her. "Stop! I don't know what's going on, but it's not *my* fault! It's those men!"

Demetrius glared at Lysander. "You've upset my Helena!" he snarled, and plunged into the woods after the women.

"Helena!" shouted Lysander. "Wait! My little fluffy pumpkin, wait!"

And he, too, joined the chase.

Oberon glared at Puck. "This is your fault," he said. "Sort it out. I'm going to find Titania."

And if I never hear the words "fluffy pumpkin" again in my entire life, he thought, *it'll be too soon.*

Chapter 7

Oberon found Titania in her favourite glade, where the wild flowers grew tall. She was sitting on a mossy bank, cradling Bottom's donkey-head in her lap, scratching him between the ears and singing him a lullaby. He'd fallen fast asleep.

Perhaps he was weary from the long night of mistakes and confusion, but Oberon didn't laugh to see his wife hugging a donkey-headed man. He didn't even smile. It didn't look funny; it looked ... sad, somehow.

Titania looked up. "Oh ... hello," she said. She sounded confused.

"Who's this?" Oberon asked, though of course he knew full well who it was. He felt a sudden stab of jealousy. All at once, he wanted to be the one who was being sung to. Above all, he wanted to never see a human ever again. Especially one who was in love with anyone else.

"Erm ... it's my Bottom," said Titania. "I'm ... er ... I seem to be in love."

"Your *Bottom*?" said Oberon. "In *love*?" You're in *love* with your *Bottom*?" Oddly, he was beginning to feel irritated, even though the whole thing was his fault.

"Yes," said Titania. "I'm ... not quite sure why. But he's lovely, isn't he?"

"No, he's not!" said Oberon crossly. "He's not lovely at all. He's a badly-dressed fat man with a donkey's head."

Titania looked down at Bottom. "Er ... yes," she said. "When you put it like that, I suppose he is. But I still seem to be in love with him." She looked at Oberon. "That doesn't really make sense, does it?"

And with that, she burst into tears.

Suddenly, Oberon felt terrible. He couldn't even remember what he and Titania had been arguing about in the first place, and now he'd made her fall in love with a silly donkey-headed man with a stupid name. He'd made everything worse, and she was crying, and it was his fault.

"There, there," he said. "Let me make it better. Just leave him alone, and come over here."

Reluctantly, Titania slipped her legs out from under Bottom's ridiculous head. Cradling it gently, she lowered it on to the mossy bank, and – looking back sadly and confusedly – followed her husband across the glade.

"Lie down here," he said, "and go to sleep. When you wake up, it'll all be better – I promise."

And as Titania closed her eyes, he began to sing a soft, dreamy song. It was the charm that would undo the magic of the little purple flower.

Meanwhile, Puck was leading Hermia, Helena, Lysander and Demetrius in a merry chase around the wood. His aim was to keep them away from one another, and to tire them out. When they were ready to sleep, he could use the flower juice to put everything right.

"Lysander!" he shouted, in perfect imitation of Demetrius's voice. "Helena's over here! And she's going to marry *me*!"

"What?" roared Lysander, following him. "She's going to marry me, not you!"

By the time Lysander reached the glade where the voice had come from, Puck was somewhere else. "Hermia, my love!" he called, now sounding just like Lysander. "I'm sorry! I need your help!"

"Lysander?" Hermia called, wiping her tears away. "I'm coming!"

But Puck was already elsewhere, and then elsewhere again. First imitating Helena's voice to call Demetrius, then pretending to be Demetrius to tease Lysander. Once again as Lysander, to plead with Hermia, then again as Hermia, to call for Helena. Round and round he led them, keeping them close to each other, but never close enough to meet, until all four of them were exhausted.

Finally, Puck led them, one by one, to a dark glade where, one by one, they fell asleep, just as he'd intended. The moon was low in the sky now, so Lysander did not see how close he was to Hermia, nor Helena how near Demetrius lay.

Bending softly over Lysander, he squeezed the juice from the little purple flower into the young man's eyes. "Sleep well," he whispered. "And when you wake, for goodness' sake, don't turn round before you've had a good long look at Hermia."

Otherwise, he thought, *I'll never hear the end of it.*

Chapter 8

Dawn was breaking when Puck returned to Oberon in the flowery glade.

"Done it, boss," he announced cheerfully. "When he wakes up, Lysander'll take one look at Hermia and fall deeply and ridiculously in love with her again. She's still in love with him, so they'll both be happy. Meanwhile, Demetrius is in love with Helena, and it's obvious that *she's* still in love with *him*. All's well that ends well, eh?"

"Excellent," Oberon said. "And the queen is no longer enchanted. Look, she's waking up."

Titania yawned, and stretched and opened her eyes. "Oberon!" she said, surprised. "Oh, I've just had the strangest dream. I dreamt I was in love with a poorly-dressed fat man with a donkey's head."

"What, like that one, you mean?" Puck said, pointing at Bottom, who was snoring away on the other side of the clearing.

"Eeeugh!" Titania shrieked. "Oh, that's *horrible*! So I didn't dream it! But how could I possibly ...?" Her voice tailed away. Oberon and Puck were suddenly very still, and very quiet, like naughty children hoping not to be told off. "There'd better be a *really* good explanation for this," she said icily.

"Oh, there is," Oberon assured her. "And I'll tell you what it is, um, later. But first ... um ... Puck! Give that poor fellow his own head back at once!"

"Right you are, boss!" Puck said, hurrying over to Bottom and removing the magical charm he'd used to transform him. The donkey-head vanished and Bottom was a man once more. "Oh, listen," Puck added. "Someone's coming!"

"I hear horses," said Titania after a moment, "and hunting horns."

Oberon sighed wearily. "I've had quite enough of humans for one night," he said. "Shall we go?"

"Agreed," said Titania. "Let's slip away, deeper into the woods. Once we're alone, perhaps you can explain exactly what's been going on."

"Certainly," answered Oberon, adding hesitantly, "and perhaps if the explanation involves, er, *someone* having been a little silly, then perhaps you might find it in your heart to forgive him?"

"Perhaps," said Titania, a small smile hidden on her lips.

And then they were gone.

The hunting party consisted of none other than Theseus,
Hippolyta and several lords and ladies. One of these lords was Egeus,
who was rather startled to find his daughter Hermia fast asleep in
a woodland clearing. Next to her, Lysander was sitting up and gazing at
her with an extremely soppy expression on his face, while across the glade
Demetrius and Helena were just waking up.

"Hermia!" Egeus said sharply. "What *are* you doing?"

"Dad!" said Hermia, waking with a start.

"Have you been out in the woods all night?"
Egeus went on. "You'll catch your death of cold!"

"Better than catching my death of Dad,"
Hermia muttered.

Theseus sighed. Obviously the running away
idea hadn't worked, and now he was going to
have to think of something else. "What's going
on?" he asked.

Lysander got to his feet, shyly glancing
at Hermia. "Well, er, your majesty, I'm really not
quite sure. You see, Hermia and I were going to
run away ..."

"*What?*" Egeus roared. "That's outrageous!
Your majesty, I demand that you throw young
Lysander in prison, or chop his head off,
or something! Do you hear that, Demetrius?
He was going to run away with Hermia!
She's supposed to be marrying *you*!"

"Um, well, about that," Demetrius said,
gazing at Helena. "I've changed my mind.
I don't want to marry Hermia. I want to
marry Helena."

"*What?*" Egeus roared again. "But ... but ...
Hermia, I *order* you to marry Demetrius!"

"Actually, Egeus," said Theseus gently, "you can't order your daughter to marry someone who doesn't want to marry her. Which," he added with sudden inspiration, "means you can't have her killed for disobeying an order you can't give her in the first place. So: take my advice, and let Hermia marry Lysander."

Lysander smiled at Hermia, and Hermia smiled at Lysander. Demetrius smiled at Helena, and Helena smiled at Demetrius. Theseus began to feel slightly queasy.

"And as for you, young Demetrius, I ... Hang on, who on earth's this?"

A round-bellied, red-nosed man was staggering towards them through the trees with a dazed but cheery expression on his face. Reaching them, he bowed clumsily before Theseus. "Your royalness!" he said. "Fancy meeting you here! Nick Bottom's the name. And, um ... my friends and I have a little play that we'd like to perform in honour of your wedding. There's a lion, but it's not a real lion, so you needn't worry that anyone's going to get eaten. And there's a lady with a beard, but he can wear a scarf over it if you like. And I'm a man. What do you say?"

"Um ... very well," said Theseus, wondering if perhaps all the people of Athens were a bit daft and he'd never noticed before. "Let me just check something. Hermia, do you still want to marry Lysander?"

Hermia smiled. "Yes, my Lord," she said.

"And, Lysander, do you want to marry Hermia?"

Lysander nodded happily.

"Demetrius, do you want to marry Helena?"

Sheepishly, Demetrius nodded. "If Helena will have me."

"Yes!" said Helena at once. "Oh, yes!"

"Right!" said Theseus. "Go and practise your play, Mr Bottom, and practise it really well. We're going to have a triple wedding, and we're going to have it today!"

"Today?" everyone chorused in surprise.

"Today," said Theseus firmly.

Because that way, he thought to himself, *we can get everyone married before anyone else changes their mind.*

And with that, he turned and – unaware of the puckish laughter that echoed through the trees around them – led the party back to Athens.

Tricks and outcomes

Problem ➡ Trick ➡ Outcome

"Oh, that woman," Oberon growled. "She makes me so cross!"

Queen Titania ... took one look at the donkey-headed Bottom, and fell deeply, and quite ridiculously, in love.

Problem ➡ Trick ➡ Outcome

"What a bunch of fools! ... Especially the red-nosed guy. He's got no more sense than a donkey."

"Er ... right," said Bottom, wondering what was going on.

Problem ➡ Trick ➡ Outcome

His aim was to keep them away from one another, and to tire them out.

Puck led them, one by one, to a dark glade where, one by one, they fell asleep.

Problem ➡ Trick ➡ Outcome

"I," Lysander said to Hermia, "will never be anyone's fluffy pumpkin but Helena's."

"Lysander, do you want to marry Hermia?" Lysander nodded happily.

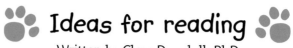

Ideas for reading

Written by Clare Dowdall, PhD
Lecturer and Primary Literacy Consultant

Learning objectives: explore the meaning of words in context; predict what might happen from details stated and implied; discuss and evaluate how authors use language, including figurative language, considering the impact on the reader; select appropriate grammar and vocabulary, understanding how such voices can change and enhance meaning; use spoken language to develop understanding through speculating, hypothesising, imagining and exploring ideas

Curriculum links: Science, Geography

Interest words: Midsummer, glade, enchantment, noble, deviously, heart-stealer, jealousy, trickster, mischievous, merriment, puzzlement

Resources: painting materials, ICT, digital camera

Getting started

This book can be read over two or more reading sessions.

- Read the blurb together. Help children to pronounce the characters' names and recognise that they are two boys and two girls.

- Focus on the phrase, "busy weaving magic and enchantment". Check that children understand what this phrase means. Using contextual information from the images and prior discussion, ask them to predict what might happen in the story.

Reading and responding

- Read through the cast list on pp2–3. Using a sticky note for each character, organise them into "fairy world" and "real world" groups, then draw lines to show how they relate to each other.

- Discuss how the characters of Egeus and Hermia are presented. Help children to make reference to the language used in the story and to draw inferences about the characters based on what is written.